MW00892313

GROUNDWOOD BOOKS HOUSE OF ANANSI PRESS TORONTO BERKELEY

Groundwood Books / House of Anansi Press
110 Spadina Avenue, Suite 801, Toronto, Ontario M5V 2K4
Distributed in the USA by Publishers Group West
1700 Fourth Street, Berkeley, CA 94710

We acknowledge for their financial support of our publishing program the Canada Council for the Arts, the Government of Canada through the Book Publishing Industry Development Program (BPIDP) and the Ontario Arts Council.

Library and Archives Canada Cataloging in Publication
Wishinsky, Frieda
Please, Louise / by Frieda Wishinsky ; illustrated by Marie-Louise Gay.
ISBN-13: 978-0-88899-796-8
ISBN-10: 0-88899-796-5
I. Gay, Marie-Louise II. Title.
PS8595.I834P54 2007 jC813'.54 C2006-905921-7

Printed and bound in China

The illustrations were done in watercolor, pencil and collage.

A special thank-you to Jacob Gay Homel for the loan of his third-grade doodles to decorate Jake's room.

For my friend, Marie-Louise Gay

FW

"Every little breeze seems to whisper Louise…"
(as sung by Maurice Chevalier and my father)

M-LG

Louise never left her brother Jake alone.

CESKA REPUBLIKA
Kč 12

She danced into his room.
She played with his toys.
She bounced on his bed.

"Go away," said Jake.
"I'm never going away," said Louise.
"Then I'll move and you'll never find me," said Jake.
"I'll find you," said Louise. "I know your name."
"I'll change my name," said Jake.

THIS
BELONGS TO:
GEORGE!

"I'll always know your face," said Louise.
"I'll wear a disguise," said Jake.
"You can't change your voice," said Louise.

"Yes, I can," growled Jake.

"You're my brother," said Louise. "You can't change that."

"Go away," said Jake, and he slammed his door shut.

Louise stood outside his room and stomped her feet.

Louise stood outside his room and pounded on his door.

Louise stood outside his room and sang, “Row, row, row your boat.”

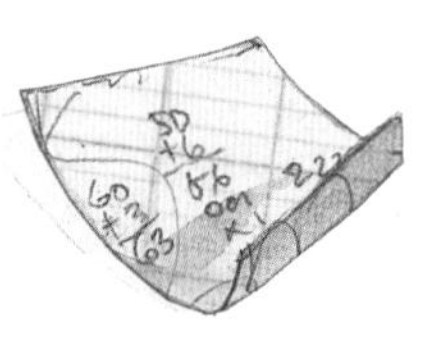

Jake scrawled GO AWAY!! on a sign and taped it to his door. "I don't have to," said Louise. "This hall is a free country."

“Well, if you won’t go away, I will,” said Jake,
and he grabbed his book and ran out the front door.
“Hey, wait for me!” shouted Louise, and she ran out the door too.

“PLEASE, Louise,” pleaded Jake. “I really want to read alone.” “But I have no one to play with,” cried Louise. “You’ll see. I’ll be quiet. You won’t even know I’m here.”

But Jake knew she was there.
Jake closed his eyes.
I wish you were a dog, he thought.

A dog wouldn't dance into his room.
A dog wouldn't pound on his door.
A dog wouldn't talk all day.
A dog wouldn't talk at all.

Why was it suddenly so quiet?
Where was Louise?
Jake looked around, but no Louise.

Jake searched the trees, the bushes and the sandbox.
No Louise.

He searched the toolshed and the birdhouse.
No Louise anywhere.

And then Jake saw a strange little dog.
The strange little dog was running toward him.
The dog was wagging its tail. The dog was licking his face.
Could it be?
"Louise?" said Jake.
"Woof!" barked the dog.

LOUISE?

"Oh no!" said Jake, and he closed his eyes.

Please, Louise.
Don't be a dog, he wished.
Please, Louise.
Come back, he wished.
Please, Louise.
Be my little sister again, he wished.

Please, Louise.

Please, Louise.

Please, Louise.

“Hi, Jake,” said Louise. “This is Billy. He just moved in next door. We want to play alone.

So Jake — GO AWAY!”

OKAY! I'M GOING!

Before he could get very far,
Louise called, “Jake! Jake!”
Jake spun around.
“See you later,” said Louise.
“See you later,” said Jake.